Bye, Bye, Butterflies!

Andrew Larsen

Illustrated by

Jacqueline Hudon-Verrelli

Fitzhenry & Whiteside

Published in Canada by Fitzhenry & Whiteside, 195 Allstate Parkway, Markham, Ontario L3R 4T8

Published in the United States by Fitzhenry & Whiteside, 311 Washington Street, Brighton, Massachusetts 02135

www.fitzhenry.ca godwit@fitzhenry.ca

10 9 8 7 6 5 4 3 2 1

Library and Archives Canada Cataloguing in Publication
Larsen, Andrew, 1960-
Bye, bye, butterflies! / Andrew Larsen ; [illustrated by] Jacqueline Hudon-Verrelli.
ISBN 978-1-55455-220-7
I. Hudon-Verrelli, Jacqueline II. Title.
PS8623.A77B94 2012   jC813'.6   C2012-901129-0

Publisher Cataloging-in-Publication Data (U.S)
Larsen, Andrew.
Bye, bye, butterflies! / Andrew Larsen ; Jacqueline Hudon-Verrelli.
[   ] p. : cm.
Summary: Inspired by the sight of some school kids releasing butterflies up into the sky, a young boy turns into a "butterfly scientist" and helps his teacher and classmates care for some caterpillars as they grow into butterflies.
ISBN: 9781554552207
1. Butterflies – Fiction – Juvenile literature. I . Hudon-Verrelli, Jacqueline. II. Title.
[E] dc23   PZ7.L3574By 2012

Fitzhenry & Whiteside acknowledges with thanks the Canada Council for the Arts, and the Ontario Arts Council for their support of our publishing program. We acknowledge the financial support of the Government of Canada through the Canada Book Fund (CBF) for our publishing activities.

Canada Council   Conseil des Arts   ONTARIO ARTS COUNCIL
for the Arts   du Canada   CONSEIL DES ARTS DE L'ONTARIO

Cover and interior design by Daniel Choi
Cover image by Jacqueline Hudon-Verrelli
Printed in Canada by Friesens

For Charlie, whose story this will always be...
With thanks to Cathy Indig and all the wonderful teachers at the MNjcc Nursery, where children grow wings.

For my parents, Charles and Marianne, and for Dario

A.L.

J.H-V.

"I like it when we're quiet," said Charlie's dad as the two of them walked down the street.

"Well, I like it better when we talk," insisted Charlie.

"But you can hear all kinds of things when you're quiet," said his dad.

"Like what?" asked Charlie.

"Listen," whispered his dad.

So Charlie listened.
And that's when he heard it.

It sounded like a chorus of children's voices.
"Yes!" the voices called out. "Yes! Bye, bye, butterflies!"

Charlie looked up at the buildings across the street.
He didn't see anything.
No children.
No butterflies.
Nothing out of the ordinary.

Then he saw something.

It was on the rooftop of the school.

He saw a single hand reach up and wave.

Then another.

And another.

He saw a butterfly emerge above the waving hands.

Then another.

And another.

They scattered.

"Bye, bye, butterflies!"

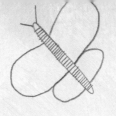
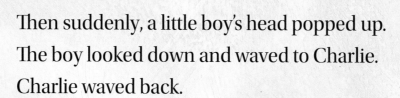

Then suddenly, a little boy's head popped up.
The boy looked down and waved to Charlie.
Charlie waved back.
"Bye, bye, butterflies!" Charlie called up to the boy.
"Bye, bye, butterflies!" the boy responded, still waving. "Bye, bye!"

And then, just like that, the boy was gone.
Just like that, the butterflies were gone.
Just like that, the sounds of the children faded.
Charlie stood alone with his dad.

"Maybe I could do something like that one day," said Charlie, hopefully.
"Maybe," said his dad, smiling.

They continued walking.

Silently.

A few months later, Charlie started school. He forgot all about the butterflies. He was too busy doing somersaults in the gym and learning to sit still during storytime.

Fall turned into winter.

And winter turned into spring.

When Charlie's class returned from spring break, a package had arrived for them.

It had a bright red sticker on it.

Inside the package were tiny jars.
Inside the jars was some special goop.
And inside the goop were teeny tiny caterpillars.

"You are all butterfly scientists now," said Miss Cathy. "Each of these tiny caterpillars will grow into a butterfly. It is your job to help them grow and to watch for the changes that take place."

"What are we going to do with them when they grow into butterflies?" asked Sophie.

"We'll let them go free," answered Miss Cathy.

Then Charlie remembered.
Bye, bye, butterflies!

Over time, the caterpillars ate the goop.

They grew and grew until they were big and fuzzy.

Then, one by one, they crawled up the sides of their jars.

One by one, they fastened themselves to the top of the jars...

...and dangled upside down.

"The caterpillars are ready to make their cocoons," Miss Cathy explained to the children. "They'll stay inside their cocoons until they have changed into butterflies."

And that's just what they did.

The next morning, the children came to school and discovered that the jars were gone. In their place was a big glass terrarium.

"Our butterflies will need more room when they come out of their cocoons," Miss Cathy explained. "Let's put some twigs and grass and flowers in the terrarium for them. It'll make things a little more cozy."

The cocoons seemed to hang around forever. The children could hardly wait.

"I know it doesn't seem like there's much going on, but it's important to keep observing," Miss Cathy reminded the children. "You never know what you might see."

After a couple of weeks, the children finally saw something...

The terrarium was a-flutter with baby butterflies.

"Our new friends will be with us for just a few days," said
Miss Cathy. "Then we will need to release them."

A few days later, it was time.

"Today's the day!" said Miss Cathy. "They're ready to go free. You've all done a great job of looking after our butterflies."

The children felt a little happy and a little sad all at once.

"I wish we could keep the butterflies forever," said Sophie.

"I know," said Charlie. "But just wait and see!"

The children gathered on the rooftop with the teachers
and the butterflies. Charlie could hardly keep still.
"Are you ready?" Miss Cathy asked the children.
"Yes!" they called out.
"Are you sure?" she asked.

"Yes!" they called out even louder.

"Then let's get ready to say good-bye," she said.

The children raised their hands and began to wave.

Miss Cathy opened the lid of the terrarium and the butterflies fluttered up, up, up and away.

"Bye, bye, butterflies!" sang the children. "Bye, bye!"

Charlie walked over to the safety rail at the edge of the rooftop. He held onto the rail and looked up at the scattering butterflies. He looked down at the sidewalk below.

A boy stood there beside his father.
The boy looked up at Charlie and waved.
Charlie waved back.
"Bye, bye, butterflies!" the boy called up.
"Bye, bye, butterflies!" Charlie responded, still waving. "Bye, bye."

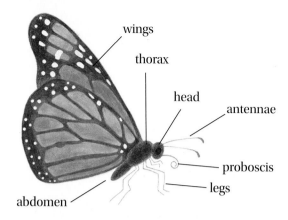

wings

thorax

head

antennae

proboscis

legs

abdomen

Are You a Butterfly or Are You a Moth?

Butterflies and moths are types of insects called *Lepidoptera*. Like all insects, they have a head, a thorax, an abdomen, two antennae, and six legs. They have four wings that are covered by scales, and a coiled proboscis for drinking liquids such as flower nectar.

- Are you brightly coloured?
- Do you fly during the day?
- Are your antennae club-shaped at the end?
- When you are resting, do you close your wings above your back?
- ⊸ If this best describes you, then you are probably a butterfly.

or

- Are you brown, grey or white?
- Do you fly at night?
- Are your antennae smooth at the end?
- When you are resting, do you spread your wings out to your side?
- ⊸ If this best describes you, then you are probably a moth.

So You Want to Be a Butterfly Scientist?

Charlie's class watched butterflies grow from caterpillars into adults. There is another way to be a butterfly scientist. You can plant a butterfly garden! It's fun! It's easy! If you plant it, they will come! There are even specially designed butterfly houses you can add as well.

Planting a butterfly garden allows you to study butterflies while providing them with a suitable habitat and helping ensure their continued conservation. Plus, it's cool to grow a garden.

Here are some flowers that butterflies will enjoy visiting in your garden.

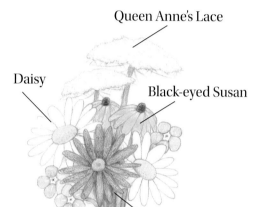

Queen Anne's Lace

Daisy

Black-eyed Susan

Forget-me-not

Aster

How to Draw Charlie

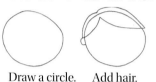

Draw a circle.   Add hair.   Add nose, eyes and mouth.   Add eyebrows. Add dots to eyes and nose.

How to Draw a Butterfly

Draw a long oval.   Add wings and antennae.   Decorate wings with spots.

Defense! Defense! Defense!

Something as delicate as a butterfly needs ways to defend itself from its enemies. Luckily, butterflies have developed a few good tricks.

The patterns and colours on the wings of some butterflies allow them to camouflage themselves and blend in with the environment. Others have "eye spots" on their wings that look like the eyes of a larger animal. It is believed that these big eyes scare off potential predators.

Some butterflies, particularly brightly coloured ones such as the monarch, are poisonous. If a predator eats a poisonous butterfly it will become violently ill. The predator will learn not to eat any more brightly coloured butterflies.

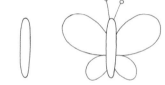

Eye spots

Life Cycle

From egg to adult, butterflies go through a series of physical transformations or changes known as **metamorphosis**. There are 4 stages of metamorphosis:

Butterfly: When the transformation is finished the adult butterfly emerges from the chrysalis. The adult butterfly will lay its eggs after mating and the whole life cycle will begin once again. (2-4 weeks)

Chrysalis: The caterpillar forms a protective shield called a chrysalis or a pupa when it has finished growing. The chrysalis attaches itself to the underside of a leaf on the host plant. Most of the transformation takes place inside the chrysalis. (1-4 weeks)

Egg: Female butterflies lay their eggs on host plants, allowing caterpillars to get their food from plant leaves. Different species of butterfly require different host plants. For instance, monarch butterflies only lay their eggs on milkweed plants. (2-4 days)

Larva: The larva or caterpillar is tiny and usually emerges from its egg after only a few days. Caterpillars spend most of their time eating the host plant and growing bigger and bigger. (2-3 weeks)

The Magnificent Migration of the Monarchs

Monarch butterflies cannot survive long, cold winters. Instead, they spend their winters in southern resting spots. Monarchs travel up to 5,000 kilometres (3,100 miles) to the same winter vacation spot year after year. Monarchs west of the Rockies travel to small groves of trees along the coast of California. **1** Monarchs east of the Rockies travel to the forests high in the mountains of Mexico. **2**

▲ Rocky Mountains

The migration of the monarch is a mysterious and awesome thing. The journey is long and it can be very dangerous.

Other migrators:
- Canada Goose
- Great White Shark
- Humpback Whale
- Polar Bear
- Robin

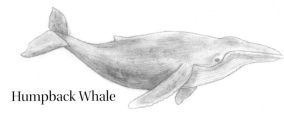
Humpback Whale

Canada Goose

Cool Facts:

- Butterflies can be found on every continent except Antarctica.
- Butterflies live in all kinds of different habitats from wetlands to meadows to urban gardens to rainforests.
- Butterflies don't eat. They drink their nourishment through a 'built-in straw' called a **proboscis**.
- There are over 20,000 species of butterflies.
- A caterpillar's first meal is its own eggshell.

- A butterfly's wing is made up of thousands of tiny scales.
- In 2009 three monarch caterpillars travelled on the space shuttle Atlantis to the International Space Station. They became the first butterflies in space.
- A grouping of butterflies can be called a **rabble**, a **swarm**, or a **kaleidoscope**.